PSYCH OUT

adapted by Mark S. Bernthal

SCHOLASTIC INC.

NEW YORK   TORONTO   LONDON   AUCKLAND   SYDNEY
MEXICO CITY   NEW DELHI   HONG KONG   BUENOS AIRES

No part of this publication may be reproduced in whole or in part, or stored in a retrieval system, or transmitted in any form or by any means, electronic, mechanical, photocopying, recording, or otherwise, without written permission of the publisher. For information regarding permission, write to Scholastic Inc., Attention: Permissions Department, 557 Broadway, New York, NY 10012.

ISBN 0-439-69112-5

Duel Masters, the Duel Masters logo, and characters' distinctive likenesses are trademarks of Wizards/Shogakukan/Mitsui-Kids. ©2005 Wizards/Shogakukan/Mitsui-Kids/ShoPro. Wizards of the Coast and its logo are trademarks of Wizards of the Coast, Inc.

HASBRO and its logo are trademarks of Hasbro and are used with permission. All Rights Reserved.

Published by Scholastic Inc.
SCHOLASTIC and associated logos are trademarks and/or registered trademarks of Scholastic Inc.

12 11 10 9 8 7 6 5 4 3 2 1   5 6 7 8 9/0

Printed in the U.S.A.
First printing, January 2005

INTRODUCTION

The world as we know it isn't the world around us. There are awesome creatures living in five mysterious civilizations, realms of Nature, Fire, Water, Light, and Darkness. They can be brought into our world through an incredible card game — Duel Masters!

Though many kids and adults play this game, only the best can call forth these creatures. They are known as *Kaijudo Masters*.

This is the story of one junior duelist, or *Senpai*, unique among all others. His name is Shobu Kirifuda.

1

Whirring helicopter propellers nearly drowned out the beep of Hakuoh's picture phone. He flipped it open to reveal the Master calling from his gloomy Temple office.

"You're returning already?" asked the Master.

"Yes," said Hakuoh. "I toyed with Toban-Jan until he was one move from winning. It's much more fun to give opponents hope, and then crush their spirits as I steal victory."

"I don't want you overexposed," said the Master,

"but you might have enjoyed the finalists dueling for the junior championship."

Hakuoh shook his head. "They're not worth watching," he replied with a smirk.

"Not even Shobu Kirifuda?" teased the Master.

"That little wannabe?" scoffed Hakuoh. "He chased me through the tournament hall, shouting challenges. Sure, he's plucky and feisty, but nothing special."

The Master's long blond hair spilled out of the hood of his robe, covering half of his sinister smile. "But the same could have been said of you once, young one."

"Should he become a real contender," said Hakuoh, "I'll crush him easily."

The Master grinned wickedly. "I have no doubt."

Back at the tournament arena, the excitement of Hakuoh's exhibition match had given way to a new brand of mayhem. Shobu's friends were so ready for the junior competition that even Rekuta Kadoko and his father, Maruo, were wearing cheerleader uniforms! Surprisingly, they didn't look much stranger than many of the duelists competing in the final rounds, but both were embarrassed by their outfits.

"Ladies and gentlemen," shouted the announcer, "the Duel Masters Battle Arena Junior Tournament is about to resume! We're down to the final 'Sweet Sixteen' duelists, one of whom will win only four more matches to be crowned champion!"

"That will be my Shobu!" said Mrs. Kirifuda proudly.

"Let me start by introducing a few of the top-scoring contenders," continued the announcer. "First, here's the prince of panache, the sultan of suave, the heir with green hair . . . let's have a warm round of applause for Toru!"

The spotlight hit the red carpet and Toru marched in, soaking up the applause like a sponge, while carefully maintaining his tough sneer.

"You know, from these seats, he doesn't look so tough," said Mr. Kadoko. "Or do I need new glasses?"

Typing stats into his laptop, Rekuta rolled his eyes. "Let's go with the latter on that one, Pop. You're lucky to see past your nose."

"And here's the king of the jungle himself . . . ," cried the announcer. "Tsuyoshi Saruyama!"

The monkey-faced little duelist stalked the red carpet on his stilts, and wowed the crowd with a forward flip dismount.

But not everyone was impressed. Shobu's cheerleaders raised cards grading Tsuyoshi's dismount a dismal 1.0.

"He lost to Shobu yesterday," grumbled Rekuta, "and they introduce him second?"

"He's dueled longer, son," said Maruo. "Show some respect."

"I'll respect him right out of the tournament if he faces Shobu again," muttered Rekuta.

Another competitor entered the auditorium. "Up next," said the announcer, "the duelist with a wicked sting! Jamira, the Viper King!"

Jamira's spiked red hair and orange and green outfit were colorful . . . to say the least!

"Hey!" shouted Sayuki. "Is this a circus or a dueling tournament? That clown switched decks on Shobu in the park the other day!"

"Viper King, my foot," said Mimi. "He's just a cheater!"

After a squawk of feedback, the announcer continued. "Next, put your hands together for twin brothers, Bobbie and Robbie, who gave up successful careers as clothes models to compete here!"

"Now we have a fashion show!" scoffed Sayuki. "Let's see a real player!"

Her demand was answered immediately. The announcer shouted, "And lastly, a duelist who's undefeated through yesterday's first rounds. Let's greet this fantastic newcomer, Shobu Kirifuda!"

As Shobu made his way to the center of the arena, the crowd went wild. He'd definitely gained some fans. His cheerleaders bounced up and down,

waving pom-poms and screaming, "Go, Shobu, go, Shobu. Go, go, *go*, Shobu. Yay!"

After the cheer, Sayuki critiqued Rekuta. "You need to kick higher," she said.

"Actually, I need therapy," moaned Rekuta, sitting down and hiding his face behind his laptop's screen.

The matchup of Toru and Tsuyoshi promised to be as interesting as it was weird. Both hoped to be in the championship match and to find Shobu there. But only one would advance to the quarterfinals.

Their contest was heated to say the least, but now Tsuyoshi was in trouble. "I summon Deathblade Beetle!" he shouted.

Unfortunately, the move was too little too late. Toru sneered. "Ha!" he exclaimed. "It's going to take more than a big bug to squash me." Then he commanded an attack. "Burning Mane! *Ike!* Break his shields!" The crowd roared, but Toru wasn't finished. "Now I call Fear Fang. *Todome da!*"

Tsuyoshi keeled over on his stilts. He was toast. Toru was moving on to the next round.

Nearby, Jamira also had his opponent — an average-looking kid named Ikito — on the ropes. "You'll never win with plain hair and clothes!" taunted Jamira. "You need exciting style, like this spell card I'm about to play. Death Smoke, nuke his blocker!"

Ikito winced, realizing the end was near.

"Time to say 'bye-bye,'" Jamira yelled. "Swamp Worm. *Todome da!*"

Ikito was history. Jamira was only three steps from the championship and the cheering crowd lifted his confidence. "I will be champion!" he shouted. He strutted and pointed to his head. "The hair will be there! I will not lose again!"

But beneath his confident crowing, Jamira was a

nervous wreck. *I can't afford to lose again!* he thought.

If he lost, he would have to face severe consequences.

A week earlier, Jamira had approached the Temple for some practice duels, but guards in hooded robes blocked his entry.

"Hey, let me in!" he demanded.

"No way," replied a guard. "You dress funny, your spiky red hair is a joke, and you leave the cap off the toothpaste!"

"Come on," objected Jamira. "What's the real reason?"

A mysterious woman, whose face was hidden by

the hood of a Temple robe, called to Jamira from the door. "You disgraced the Temple when you lost to Shobu Kirifuda," she explained. "You couldn't even beat him by cheating."

"He got lucky!" exclaimed Jamira. "Give me another chance! No way will he beat me again."

He tried to push past the guards, but they shoved him to the ground.

"Let me talk to the Master," pleaded Jamira. "He'll back me up."

"Defeat Shobu Kirifuda at the Duel Masters Junior Tournament next week," replied the woman, "and you'll be allowed back into the Temple. Don't ever return if you lose!" Then she slammed the enormous door with a loud crash.

4

Shobu defeated his first opponent quickly, and advanced to the quarterfinals. His current opponent was a weird, geeky dude called The Brain. A typically flamboyant duelist, he wore thick glasses, a lime green sport coat, purple pants, and polka-dot bow tie. Regardless of wardrobe, Shobu always focused on an opponent's skills. And he'd seen enough to know The Brain's game was lame!

"Bolshack Dragon. *Ike!* Attack!" shouted Shobu. Then he delivered the knockout punch. "And now, Brawler Zyler, *todome da!*"

The Brain went insane, staggering backward with his bow tie spinning. Shobu was a semifinalist. He'd made the final four!

His personal cheering section erupted. "Shobu, Shobu ruled the duel! He just took The Brain to school! *Go, Shobu!*"

Nearby, the ever-cool Knight nodded with grudging appreciation for the cheer. *They're getting better,* he thought.

By now many girls thought Shobu was the cutest new duelist. A group of them shouted their own cheer. "Shobu, Shobu! He's so hot! He just showed us what he's got! *Go, Shobu!*"

"Hey!" Mimi objected, feeling a little jealous. "That's not an authorized Shobu cheer! And they're not wearing official Shobu cheerleader uniforms!"

Still embarrassed, Rekuta muttered, "I've got one they can have."

His father nodded. "Me, too."

The first semifinal match pitted Jamira against Shobu. Rekuta checked his laptop's database and quickly reminded everyone that Jamira used Nature cards effectively.

"Not as effectively as he switches decks before a duel!" added Sayuki sarcastically.

Down on the arena floor, the same thought occurred to Shobu as he shuffled his cards. "Plan on cheating again, Jamira?"

"Don't have to," replied the obnoxious redhead. "I've done my homework."

"Think you know my deck, huh?" asked Shobu.

Fearing the Master's judgment, Jamira had studied much more than Kirifuda's duelist moves. He'd spied on Shobu in school, after school, in the dueling park, and even in his home! Then he concocted plans to put Shobu off balance.

"Oh, I know a lot more about you than your passion for Bolshack Dragon," Jamira replied with a sly grin. "I have multiple strategies to mess with your head."

"Multiple strategies, huh?"

"Yep," said Jamira, "the first is called 'No Detention, please.'"

Shobu was puzzled as Jamira turned and waved at a sweet little old lady in the front row. He called to her in a devilish tone. "Oh, Miss Crumbcrock, wave to Shobu!"

Miss Crumbcrock popped up excitedly, waved her cane, and shouted, "Shobu, Shobu! You're my boy! Treat Jamira like a toy! *Go, Shobu!*"

"Another unauthorized cheer," grumbled Mimi. "Competition is spreading."

"What are you going to do?" Sayuki asked Mimi sarcastically. "Send Miss Crumbcrock to cheerleader detention?"

Hearing the schoolteacher's support for Shobu, Jamira's jaw dropped. He adjusted his vest nervously. "But . . . but . . . you . . . you can't duel in front of her! I saw! She slaps you with detention if you even think about your cards in her class!"

"Oh, that's only in school," said Shobu. "Outside class, Miss Crumbcrock is one of my biggest fans. We duel in detention. If you're not careful, she can drown you with her wicked Water deck. Got any other surprises for me?"

Jamira gritted his teeth and growled, "You bet, loser. I have more tricks up my sleeve."

"That would be great," said Shobu, "if your shirt had sleeves."

S hields ready. *Ikuzo!*" shouted Shobu.

"Deploy shields. *Koi!*" Jamira answered.

Jamira opened with a bold move. "I call this strategy 'What a Waste,'" he said with a cackle. He used Shobu's favorite card, Bolshack Dragon, to charge mana.

The crowd *ooed*. Shobu's friends *aahed*.

Jamira just snickered weirdly. "What are you going to do now that I've turned your favorite card into mana?"

Shobu calmly answered the move. "Well, I guess I'll turn *this* card into mana," he said.

Rekuta frantically typed the move into the duel log. "Oh my gosh! Shobu's also used Bolshack Dragon as mana!"

Flabbergasted, Jamira shouted, "Hey! What's the matter with you? You don't want to use that card as mana."

"Why not?" Shobu replied calmly. "You did."

"But . . . but . . . but that's my strategy," he stammered. "You can't steal it!"

"Take it as a compliment," said Shobu.

Knight smiled, adjusting his sunglasses. *Impressive counter move,* he thought. *The kid can really think on his feet.*

"The match has really taken a turn," said Mr. Kadoko.

"I think Shobu's lost his mind, wasting Bolshack Dragon like that," moaned Rekuta.

"Relax and keep typing," said Sayuki. "It was a cool copycat move and Shobu has a plan."

Out of the blue, Mimi inquired, "What rhymes with dragon?"

"Why do you ask, dear?" asked Shobu's mom.

"We need an appropriate cheer," Mimi answered.

Shobu now had Onslaughter Triceps and the double breaker power of Gatling Skyterror in play. Jamira saw the match slipping away, despite his secret strategies. He made one last effort to psych Shobu into defeat, intertwining his arms and raising them in the air. Then he gyrated, twisted, and wiggled his body, all the while staring hypnotically into Shobu's eyes.

The crowd howled with laughter, but Miss Crumbcrock quickly grew impatient. "What is this?" she shouted. "A belly dance or a duel? Play your cards, you deadhead redhead!"

"Wow!" Rekuta exclaimed. "Miss Crumbcrock is never that cool when she's teaching social jurisprudence!"

"But why is Jamira wiggling like a worm?" wondered Rekuta's dad.

"He looks more like a snake," countered Shobu's mom. "I don't like snakes around my son."

Rekuta quickly scanned his database. "It's Jamira's Viper Dance! Says here that some believe he hypnotizes opponents with it. Other analysts think it just bores the competition to death. Either way, the opposing duelist's brain is fried, and Jamira wins the duel."

Jamira saw that his slithering and snakelike gaze was affecting Shobu. "While studying with duelists in Tibet," he said, "I learned how cobras lure frogs to their deadly fangs."

A blank expression fell over Shobu's face and his eyes glazed over. "I am not a frog," he mumbled in a slow monotone.

Jamira wriggled and stared even harder. "But you feel like one, don't you?"

"Yes," Shobu admitted, nodding his head slowly.

Rekuta studied the scene below. "What are we going to do, Pop?"

Mr. Kadoko's eyes were glazed, too. "I . . . feel . . . like a frog," he answered slowly.

"Not the advice we were looking for!" said Rekuta.

"Your mind is growing weak under my spell," Jamira chanted to Shobu. "You are confused. You can no longer duel."

Come on, kid, Knight thought. *Snap out of it. Believe in yourself!*

Deep in Shobu's mind, he heard a voice repeating

a single phrase. "Believe in yourself. Believe in yourself." The voice grew louder and louder.

Jamira could see that Shobu was fighting his spell and tried to finish him off before he could snap out of it. "You can no longer duel," he intoned in a steady, commanding voice. "You must forfeit the match. You believe me, don't you?"

"I believe in myself!" Shobu suddenly shouted. His eyes popped open. He'd broken the trance and was ready to rock. "And no sneaky strategy is better than a quick attack! Gatling Skyterror! *Ike!* Double break his shields! Triceps, attack! *Todome da!*"

Jamira the Viper had just been defanged.

Shobu would duel Toru for the championship.

Jamira slithered away, defeated. "With all my Tibetan training," he mumbled, "how could I lose?"

"When it comes to winning," answered Shobu, "nothing beats hard work and determination."

The crowd roared. A group of girls cheered, "We love Shobu! True romance! He just beat the Viper Dance! Go, Shobu!"

Mimi sighed. "Another unauthorized cheer, but they're good," she admitted. "If we can't beat 'em, maybe we should join 'em."

Best news I've heard in a while, thought Knight.

8

Shobu and his pals waited for the final match in a room beneath the arena. Sayuki and Mrs. Kirifuda paced nervously. Rekuta scanned his computer for more data on Toru. Mimi frantically tried to invent more cheers. Over in a corner, Miss Crumbcrock practiced kung-fu moves with her cane.

Shobu was playing it cool. Maybe too cool. "What are you worried about?" he said calmly. "No way am I going to lose the championship duel."

"Don't be overconfident," Sayuki chided. "It makes you careless."

"She's right," declared Mr. Kadoko. "Terrible trouble comes in many disguises."

Immediately, trouble entered the room in a terrible disguise. Unfortunately, the group was too preoccupied to recognize Jamira, who was wearing a pink dress, a wide brimmed hat, makeup, and a horrible shade of lipstick. He tottered unsteadily in high heels, and carried a tray of canned soft drinks.

In a squeaky voice, Jamira said, "I'm a big fan of Shobu's, so I brought his favorite soft drink, Gagalot Cola! I thought you'd want some refreshment before the big duel."

"Wow!" exclaimed Shobu. "Gagalot? Thanks a lot!"

"You're gaga-welcome," squeaked Jamira. Then he quickly left. No one noticed his satisfied sneer under his horrible shade of lipstick.

Shobu pounded down two cans of Gagalot in seconds. He wiped his lips and burped loudly. "See? The public has spoken. I'll be the people's duelist.

Everyone will like me, and my deck will be encased in the Smithsonian."

Sayuki rolled her eyes. "Oh, gaga-please! Lose the big head, Kirifuda. Toru's a great duelist, too."

Shobu chugged his third Gagalot, then shook the rafters with a blasting belch.

"If your nerves don't give you the shakes," said his mother, "all that sugar will!"

"I found something that might give Shobu the jitters," said Rekuta. "My research says Toru's deck is a combination of Water and Nature cards, but he doesn't seem to have a trump card, like Shobu does with Bolshack Dragon."

"Maybe he doesn't use one," commented Sayuki.

"Or he's held it back to surprise you in the championship duel!" added Mr. Kadoko. "Either way, I've watched Toru at my card shop since Kokujo destroyed him that day. His deck has definitely evolved for the better since then."

"Let's hope it isn't *evolving* in his waiting room right now!" declared Rekuta.

"Toru acts tough," answered Sayuki, "but I don't think he's a cheater."

"Well, the match will start soon," said Mrs. Kirifuda. "Let's give Shobu some time to himself."

As they left the room, Miss Crumbcrock shouted, "Rule the duel, Shobu! Or it's detention all next week!"

Excitement ran through the arena, as the "official" cheerleading squad shouted, "Shobu, Shobu, he's our man! If he can't do it, no one can! *Go, Shobu!*"

That was answered quickly by the "unofficial" cheerleaders. "We just think it's really sad. Your Shobu cheers are very bad! *Go, Shobu!*"

Rekuta slumped, embarrassed. "This is getting worse, Pop."

"So true," mumbled Mr. Kadoko.

Mimi's cell phone rang.

Rekuta brightened. "Great! Cheering interrupted."

Mimi spoke on the phone for a bit, and then snapped it shut. "Um . . . I have to go," she said.

"Are you kidding?" asked Sayuki. "Shobu's biggest match ever is about to start!"

"Sorry," Mimi apologized. Then she darted up the arena steps toward an exit.

"She's probably going to negotiate a merger with the 'unofficial' cheerleaders," mumbled Rekuta.

"Anything that'll get us out of these outfits is fine with me," replied his dad.

10

Toru sat alone in a different waiting room, flipping through his deck and mentally reviewing each card. *Use it. Use it. Don't use it. Use it.*

He was interrupted by a knock on the door. Toru expected a tournament official, but was surprised by a mysterious woman. She wore a hooded cloak that covered her face, looking quite like the person who'd banished Jamira from the Temple a week earlier.

"I bring you an order from the Master," she whispered, holding out a duelist's deck. "You will abandon your deck for the final match and use this one which we have chosen for you."

"Why?" asked Toru, shocked.

"The Master doesn't believe you can defeat Shobu with your deck," answered the stranger.

"No way!" cried Toru. "Changing a deck mid-tournament is forbidden! It's cheating!"

"Those I represent have the power to bend the rules," the woman said calmly. "Now take it. This is an exact replica of Mr. Hakuoh's Light Civilization deck. Use it and you'll win."

Toru frowned as he thought about the offer.

The cloaked woman placed the new deck on the

table next to him. "Pick up the cards and learn to follow orders. This is the will of the Temple. If you obey, you'll be much better off. If you don't, you'll be expelled from the Temple."

"Do you know how long it took me to build my own deck?" muttered Toru. "And now you say I can't use it? What kind of a quitter do you think I am?"

"I'll be watching you," said the woman. "Obey the Temple and use this deck. You want to be champion, don't you?"

The woman left the room quietly, leaving Toru glancing back and forth at the two decks on the table.

11

Shobu studied his own deck in deep thought. *Toru's probably hiding his trump card,* he realized. *What kind of strategy wouldn't need one? Either way, I won't cheat by changing my deck. Better to play for fun than try to win at any cost. Besides, I believe in my deck and I'm ready to rumble!*

But Shobu's stomach was ready to rumble, too! Suddenly all that Gagalot Cola raised a ruckus. He needed a men's room. Fast!

Shobu bolted from the waiting room and dashed up the hallway.

Still wearing a pink dress, Jamira emerged from a dark corner and wobbled up the hallway in pursuit of Shobu. He'd barely learned to walk in high heels, let alone run in them!

"Welcome to the Junior Duelists Championship Match, ladies and gentlemen," shouted the announcer. "It's time now to meet our final two contestants! With the funny green hair and villainlike demeanor . . . welcome Toru Kamiya!"

Toru marched up the red carpet in the spotlight, waving to his fans.

"New to the tournament scene, this young man is a surprising finalist!" the announcer continued. "Let's welcome a talented player with even funnier hair — Shobu Kirifuda!"

The spotlight flashed on the arena entrance and the crowd went wild.

But the rabid cheers soon hushed to an eerie silence.

Where was Shobu?

12

Hands tied behind his back, Shobu lay on the men's room floor. Jamira cackled uncontrollably as he stole Shobu's dueling deck.

"It's payback time, Kirifuda. Too bad you like Gagalot Cola as much as winning duels. This is where you really belong! In the toilet! Now you'll be a loser, just like you made me!"

A strong hand gripped Jamira's wrist, forcing him to drop the cards.

It was Knight to the rescue!

"Just because you lost, doesn't mean you have to

stay a loser," Knight told Jamira. "Now show some character and untie Shobu. He has a championship to win, while you go home and figure out how to beat him next time you duel."

Sayuki and Rekuta returned to the arena seats. "We went in opposite directions," said Rekuta, "but we couldn't find Shobu anywhere."

"Oh, no!" cried Shobu's mom. "The judge is approaching the microphone. They're going to dis-qualify Shobu!"

"Wait!" screamed Shobu. He dashed into the arena, "Wait! I'm here! Let's duel!"

The crowd went wild as both competitors took their places across from each other. Shobu placed his deck on the table. "Okay, Toru. Let's keep this match fair and square. Let me see the deck you've built that will destroy me!"

Toru reached into his right pocket, then hesitated. Then he pulled a deck from the left pocket. Each shuffled the other's deck and the match was on.

Shobu opened by charging mana. Toru did the same with a Water Civilization card.

From a dark corner of the arena, the mysterious woman shook her head. Toru had disobeyed the Master and was playing with his own deck.

Shobu then charged mana and summoned Immortal Baron, Vorg.

"I charge mana," Toru answered, "and summon Aqua Vehicle."

Rekuta typed the duel moves into his database. "Toru's card has only one thousand power," he said. "Shobu should defeat it easily."

Shobu did just that. "I charge mana and summon

Brawler Zyler! Immortal Baron, Vorg! *Ike!* Break his shields!"

Toru had lost a shield, but quickly countered. "I summon Bronze-arm Tribe."

Sayuki was impressed. "Smooth move by Toru," she said. "His increased mana will come in handy. Shobu better be careful."

13

As the matched progressed, Shobu looked strong. He used Fatal Attacker Horvath to bring Toru's remaining shields down to two.

Miss Crumbcrock liked what she saw, rising to cheer, "Shobu, Shobu, he's our man! You won't beat him! No one can!"

But Toru didn't agree with her. "Don't be so sure you're winning, Kirifuda. Here comes my secret strategy. Aqua Vehicle, I give you new life! Evolve into Crystal Paladin!"

"Whoa!" shouted Rekuta. "Crystal Paladin is huge! Shobu's never played against evolution creatures."

"This could be his greatest challenge," said Sayuki.

Toru immediately attacked with Crystal Paladin, destroying Immortal Baron, Vorg. "After Kokujo humiliated me," said Toru, "I've struggled to uncover the secret of evolution creatures. And now I've succeeded. With this creature, I'll become the best duelist!"

Shobu remained calm. "I'll now use Magma Gazer to power up Fatal Attacker Horvath to now defeat Crystal Paladin. Surprised, Toru?"

Toru nodded with respect.

"You're a worthy opponent, Toru," said Shobu, "and you've played fair and square. But my deck is stronger."

Toru smiled. "I'll show you the unstoppable powers of an evolved deck. Now, Burning Mane!"

"I suppose that one will evolve, too?" Shobu guessed.

"You got it," replied Toru. "I can also evolve the creature with this card!"

"Great Kaiju, what is that?" shouted Shobu.

"Meet Fighter Dual Fang," explained Toru confidently. "He has a double-breaker capability, with power of eight thousand! And with no summoning sickness, he attacks! *Ike!*"

Rekuta typed frantically. "Yikes! He just blew away two of Shobu's shields!"

"This looks bad," Sayuki said. "Maybe Toru is stronger."

14

Shobu remained calm and made his next move. "Tornado Flame, shield trigger!"

"Give up, Kirifuda," taunted Toru. "No Fire Civilization card can defeat the eight thousand power of Fighter Dual Fang."

"We'll see," said Shobu. "I summon Immortal Baron, Vorg."

"That card has only two thousand power, Shobu," Toru pointed out. "You're getting sloppy."

"That wasn't my trump card," said Shobu. "I now

summon Rothus the Traveler! Bye-bye, Fighter Dual Fang."

The crowd cheered Shobu's creativity against powerful, evolved creatures.

Toru was far from finished. "I still have mana and all the creatures I need, Shobu!" he screeched. "With nothing to lose, I'm most psychotic. Prepare to be crushed. Marine Flower! Aqua Hulcus! Fear Fang! *Ike!*"

"Three against one?" said Shobu's mom, with a gasp. "Is that fair?"

"Numbers aren't always important," said Sayuki. "Shobu trusts his cards."

Shobu didn't seem bothered at all. "I summon Bolshack Dragon!" he called. "Rothus the Traveler! *Ike!*"

"Toru only has one shield left!" cheered Sayuki. "Shobu can win!"

Toru paused to think through the situation. *I only need this one shield. I have two blockers. Shobu*

can't destroy me. Then he attacked. "Aqua Hulcus! *Ike!* Fear Fang! *Ike!*"

A hush fell over the crowd as they waited to see how Shobu would react to this attack.

Toru smiled smugly, sure he'd won. "Didn't like that, did you?" he asked. "Ready to surrender, Shobu?"

"Not when I'm holding a Fire Civilization card that destroys all blockers," replied Shobu. "Meet Scarlet Skyterror!"

Blocker cards blown away, Toru's lone shield was unprotected.

Shobu finished him. "Bolshack Dragon! Take the championship! *Ike!*"

15

The crowd went berserk.

The announcer shouted, "The winner and supreme champion is Shobu Kirifuda!"

Shobu's closest fans hugged each other happily as Mimi returned to the group.

"Did I miss anything?" she asked.

"Just the greatest match Shobu's ever played!" answered Sayuki.

Nearby, the "unofficial" cheerleaders shouted, "We've all jumped on Shobu's wagon! Shobu is our Bolshack Dragon! *Go*, Shobu!"

Mimi slumped and dropped her pom-poms. "*Now* I know what rhymes with dragon."

Down on the arena floor, Shobu nodded respectfully to Toru. "Terrific duel," he said. "Your evolution creatures are great. And you played fair and square."

"But I lost," Toru replied sourly.

"Dueling's all about having fun," said Shobu. "Nothing else matters."

"Yeah," Toru agreed. "Having fun and making new friends."

"And making new friends," repeated Shobu in agreement. He stuck out his hand for Toru to shake.

Toru shook it, smiling.

16

The Master's dismal office was the perfect atmosphere to complement his sinister personality. The candlelight barely revealed the mysterious woman finishing her report.

"So Toru defied your order and played with his own deck," she said. "But his skill with evolution creatures was impressive."

The Master nodded and considered what he'd heard. "Toru may have promise after all. As for Shobu Kirifuda, he has a gift. I've decided to invite him to the Temple."

Get the inside edge!

Look for D-MAX membership offers
in the Duel Masters Starter Set
or check online at Duelmasters.com

DUEL MASTERS

TRADING CARD GAME